T0147113

COSMIC WARRIOR

Raymond J. Henry

BALBOA.
PRESS
A DIVISION OF HAY HOUSE

Balboa Press books may be ordered through booksellers or by contacting:

Balboa Press
A Division of Hay House
1663 Liberty Drive
Bloomington, IN 47403
www.balboapress.com
1 (877) 407-4847

Because of the dynamic nature of the Internet, any web addresses or links contained in this book may have changed since publication and may no longer be valid. The views expressed in this work are solely those of the author and do not necessarily reflect the views of the publisher, and the publisher hereby disclaims any responsibility for them.

The author of this book does not dispense medical advice or prescribe the use of any technique as a form of treatment for physical, emotional, or medical problems without the advice of a physician, either directly or indirectly. The intent of the author is only to offer information of a general nature to help you in your quest for emotional and spiritual well-being. In the event you use any of the information in this book for yourself, which is your constitutional right, the author and the publisher assume no responsibility for your actions.

Any people depicted in stock imagery provided by Getty Images are models, and such images are being used for illustrative purposes only. Certain stock imagery © Getty Images.

Print information available on the last page.

ISBN: 978-1-9822-1575-0 (sc)
ISBN: 978-1-9822-1576-7 (e)

Balboa Press rev. date: 11/08/2018

Contents

Unlike anyone else, Carter had powers that would be straight out of an adventure comic book series. He long ago decided they were his cross to bear. He had flight, super strength and enhanced reflexes. He wanted to use these powers to right the wrongs of the world and take revenge on those who orphaned him at such a young age, but he has not yet been able to track them down but knew that somehow, sometime, he would.

"They...they're fine...I can feel them growing inside me, but I have not had any trouble controlling them." Laura's expression grew to one of concern. Though he was not related by blood, she thought of him as she would her own son if she would have had one. "Carter, you know you can tell me anything, right? If you find yourself having trouble with your powers or anything unrelated to your powers.... if you just need to talk about anything, I am here for you." Carter assured her that he knew she was there for him but that he was fine. Just then they heard the pitter patter of little feet coming down the stairs. A little girl, around 11 years old, came running into the kitchen and grabbed a toaster pastry. This was Hope, Laura's youngest daughter. She was a brilliant young lady, always wanting to learn and constantly shocking her mother with her level of maturity and intelligence. She is in the same grade as Carter and her big sister, Maria. "Morning squirt" Carter teased. Hope looked over at him with a big grin, "Morning Carter"!

Hope asked Laura if she was still allowed to go work with her today and Laura smiled and assured her that yes, she was going with her today. Carter ruffled Hope's hair and told her not to push any big red buttons. Hope giggled and turned to talk to Laura. Carter watched her and thought to himself what a happy little girl she was living in such a messed-up world. Laura was already so proud of Hope and Hope had not even started working with her yet, but she reminded Hope that this wasn't a real day at work, just a job shadow day, you are lucky I could get one of my scientists to sign off on it. Yes, Mama Hope replied. Hope hugged her mom and went to watch TV.

Laura was the head of Hall Industries, her own company she started after her husband left them shortly after Hope was born. Carter never met him and was OK with that. Hope was dead set on working for Laura after she got out of school. Carter felt he needed to remined Laura that Hope would never leave her side, but Laura already knew that. "I know, she said, and it worries me because I am not going to be around forever, what will she do when I am gone?" This thought bothered Carter more than he would care to admit, he said "I don't know but I have to get going". "See you later." He ran outside and flew off. He was getting pretty good at this flying thing. He also knew Laura was becoming concerned with him.

Back at the house Laura's oldest daughter Maria walked into the kitchen and poured herself some cereal." Good morning" she said tiredly. She looked around wondering where Carter was, he always beat her downstairs in the morning. "Good morning back" Laura said and kissed Maria on the forehead." Carter already left, he did not say where he was going." Maria looked down, she was a little upset that Carter kept leaving without letting anyone know where he was going or even telling her good-bye. It all started when he went after a lead on the gang that killed his family. It could only mean that he was close to finding the leader of the gang which did not sit well with Laura or Maria. "He can't keep doing this, is he really on the right track to finding that gang Maria asked worriedly." Laura responded in a comforting voice while stroking her hair "I am not sure Maria, but I do know he is not a dumb kid, he is smart and will not do anything dangerous or stupid." Laura's voice sounded confident for Maria's sake, but she has never felt more doubtful about a situation than she was about this one.

messing up my car and my boys." He grabbed a baseball bat out of his car as Carter tried to get up. He slammed the bat down onto Carters back and Carter let out a painful cry. "You think you're a big man, kid? You think your tough? Your nothing but a punk." He struck Carter again. Carter growled through his teeth, "you killed my parents, my brothers, I have nobody now because of you." The leader struck Carter again. "That wasn't my fault kid, your old man just wasn't good at paying his debt." Carter turned to face him when the bat came down again but this time he caught it. "Don't you DARE talk about my father, he was a good man that would never get involved with the likes of you." The leader tried to pull the bat away, but Carter's grip was too much for him. The leader pulled as hard as he could, and Carter kicked him into an old gas station that was abandoned after the "Steele Vipers" moved into the neighborhood. The leader raised his gun and pointed it at Carter just as Carter noticed one of the tanks leaking gasoline. Carter ran towards him yelling for him to stop, trying to warn him about the leak but it was too late, the leader fired the gun. Carter dodged the bullet, but the gunfire ignited the fumes and the whole place went up in flames, the explosion threw Carter into the street. He got up and stared at the flames and realized there was nothing he could do to save the leader of the gang. He flew away to a quiet place to process what had just happened. He had never witnessed anyone die before. Later that night he snuck into the manor through the back door but before he could go upstairs, the kitchen lights turned on and Laura was sitting at the table in her pajamas with a cold plate of food she had prepared for him. Carter inhaled sharply and exhaled softly as he walked over and slowly sat down in the chair beside her. They sat there in silence for what seemed like an eternity to Carter and then Laura spoke. "Your hurt, is that because you found the gang leader? Did you have anything to do with what happened at that abandoned gas station earlier today?" Carter looked up at her with his slightly bruised face. "Laura…. I…. I didn't mean to kill him…it wasn't my fault. He grabbed his gun and I tried to stop him but when he fired, it ignited the fumes and the whole place went up, it all happened so fast…...I just didn't have time." Laura tilted her head a bit and said, "I thought you wanted him dead". Carter took a minute and said, "I thought I did too but, now I just feel regret." Laura got up and rubbed his shoulders. "That is not a bad thing Carter, it means you still have morals and feelings, sympathy and empathy. I am sorry for the night you just had, I know his death does not make you feel better like you thought it would." She slowly pushed his plate in front of him and took his jacket off to look at the bruises. They were dark and painful to look at, but she knew he would be fine after a little rest. Light bruising usually disappeared very quickly for him and there was no way to know what they looked like when he first got them, she realized she probably did not want to know. After he ate, he went to his room and went to bed and slept a very fitful sleep.

Healing

The next day, Maria was the first to wake up. She peered into Carters room to make sure she did not miss him, he was still asleep in his bed. Laura had turned off his alarm clock to let him rest and heal. Laura went downstairs to make some bacon and eggs for everyone but especially for Carter, she thought it would help the healing process, mentally and physically. Later in the morning, Laura saw Carter leave his room limping and in pain. She grabbed his shoulder in one hand and his wrist in the other. "Carter, you need to rest, you are in no condition to be up walking around." He shrugged her off and went down stairs without a word. Carter sat down beside Maria and began to eat his breakfast and caught Maria staring at his bruises. As she looked at them, she saw them slowly healing before her eyes. As Carter straightened his back, the pain started to subside with the bruising. "Carter", Maria said under her breath, he looked over at her and rested his head on her shoulder as she rubbed his back. "I am glad you're OK. "I am glad too" he said and smiled." They both unknowingly grabbed each other's hands and Maria rested her head on his head which was resting on her shoulder. Laura could not help herself, she took out her phone and took a picture. She could not help but wonder how Maria was able to calm him just by being near, she really was good for him. It was like they needed each other more than they knew. A phenomenon Laura saw a few years after Carters power awoke. Carter could also sense when Maria was upset about something and always knew just how to help her.

droid designs. "You have been busy Hope, I have been wondering what was in the encrypted file, my records indicate it was accessed earlier today but I did not see you here, perhaps there was an error, or you allowed some one access." Hope looked at Shep and asked if he knew who it was. Shep asked for a minute to check the security footage. "Ah, said Shep, it was Arthur Hart, he seems to be taking pictures of your work." Hope started to panic and ran to get Laura. Mom, some guy named Arthur Hart hacked into my encrypted file and was taking pictures of my blue prints. Laura looked puzzled, are you sure? He is one of my best employees, are you sure it was him? Hope nodded. Ok Shep, Laura said, let's see what Arthur has been up to. He could have been paid a lot of money to steal my work for my competitors. Laura continued working on her current project while Shep searched for more footage of Arthur. A half an hour later, Shep came back with the results they were looking for. "Miss Laura, Mr. Hart has been placing a lot of calls to the United States Military and he has also stated that he will be missing work Thursday for a check-up, but his medical records indicate he is not due at the doctor's office for another 2 months." Laura slammed her fist down on the desk, I swear if he is making weapons for the Army I am going to......she remembered Hope was standing there so she stopped to regroup and said...." fire him". Later that night they went home, and Hope walked up to Carter. "Um, Carter, can I ask you something?" Sure, I guess, he replied. Hope shared what she knew about Arthur Hart. "Ok, well, what do you want me to do honey, I can't just go beat him up because he stole your ideas." Hope frantically waved her hands, "No ... don't beat him up! I just want you to go to the military testing site not far from here. I did some digging and saw that he was heading there Thursday." Carter crossed his arms. How many systems did you have to hack to come up with this info? Hope put her hands behind her back, ashamed of herself, kind of. A couple, she replied, his phone and his laptop. Carter sighed and patted her head. "I guess I will do it." She squealed with glee and hugged him tightly. "Thank you so much Carter." Carter smiled and hugged her back and then went to bed.

to me Carter...you are not ready to be some costumed hero, out
to save the world. You need training before you can do anything
a superhero would do and since I do not know any superheroes I
would not know where to start looking for someone to train you.
Not to mention you have school to focus on." Carter did not like
what she was saying. "Whatever, it's not like I need armor to be a
superhero AND it's not like you can stop me." Laura fired back
yelling." Yes, I can..... you are not going to go out and risk your
life like a fool." His reply broke her heart. "It's not like you are my
mother!" As soon as he said it, he regretted it. he went pale as did
Laura. Neither one of them could believe what he just said and
Hope and Maria, who were listening upstairs were just as shocked.
Laura choked up a little when she was finally able to speak. "Well,
right now young man, I am glad I am not." Tears filled Carters
eyes, "I just want to help people." and with that, he ran up the stairs
and into his room. "Carter wait, I am so sorry, Carter please, come
back." Laura went to his bedroom door and tried to open it, but it
was locked...she knocked but he would not open it. She leaned her
head against the door for what seemed like hours before she finally
turned around and went back downstairs to start dinner. Later
that night, Carter finally came out of his room and he looked down
to see a pile of clothes on the floor with a note on top that read
"Carter, if you are really set on helping people, I guess I really can't
stop you, but please be safe and wear these, Love Laura". He put
the note in his pocket and picked up the clothing. It was a type of
Kevlar armor but much stronger and much lighter and a lot more
flexible, so his movements would not be hindered. He went back
to his room and tried it on. It was thick and hard on the outside,
but the inside breathed and felt comfortable as did the mask. It had
a small slit in the eyes and it was made of a much thinner version
of the suit. Carter thought to himself "how long has she had this
thing"? It fit perfectly. Guess she had it on standby for me after that

stunt at the gas station with the gang leader. He beat the chest of the armor and he could feel the impact spread throughout the body of the suit, but it did not reach his body. He did some stretches and his movements were not hindered at all. When he removed the suit, he laid it in his closet and went to bed to get some rest, so he could get up early to check out the military base the next day like he promised Hope.

After school the next day, Carter went to the base with a modified gaming headset Hope gave him, so they could talk. When he got to the testing site, he saw a droid modified from Hope's original design. The droid was walking around the area. There's a big robot, no wait, it's your droid. "Hey, I found your droid and it has weapons. "Hope, how big was this thing supposed to be?" Hope growled, "What weapons? It was only supposed to be about as big as me. Why?" Carter looked carefully and hovered towards the droid to get a good look at it. "Well, it's as big as a building, and I see..... machine guns and missile launchers. How long ago did you start this thing?" Hope thought about it a little while before answering "about 8 or 9 month ago." Carter told her that he thinks Arthur must have accessed it at the very beginning since he was able to add weapons to it so quickly. As the droid was walking around it looked up at Carter and its optics turned red. "Uh, I think its angry......oh yeah, it's definitely angry." Carter looked over at the observation building and started waiving his hands trying to get their attention to tell them to shut the weapons down. In the observation building they were looking at him with binoculars. Arthur asked General Lyndon "Who or what is that guy?" General Lyndon responded with "Whatever it is, it's in restricted air space. Seems like the perfect test subject for our little weapon." Arthur got very nervous. Meanwhile, Hope was looking through her blueprints for any weak spots and blind spots that could help Carter. "Carter, the joints of the legs and neck are some areas you can target, they are weaker than the rest." Carter was a little busy dodging machine gun fire from the droid. "They are protected, I can't hit them. Maybe it has a blind spot under its belly." He flew down and soon realized it had auto turrets on the bottom. He flew out frantically, "Nope, not a safe area either." He flew up higher to gain distance, but the droid prepped its missiles and launched four of them at him. "Hope, missile countermeasures please!" He asked frantically. "Uhm…fly through the center of their path." Carter flew straight through them and they turned to chase him. Two of the missiles collided and the other two were sent into a spiral to the ground where they exploded. Carter landed on top of the droid and ran his hands along his leg until he found a joint plate and ripped it up to hide under it. Arthur was starting to sweat as he realized he did not make defenses in the joints. Just then the front left leg of the droid fell off and the whole thing toppled over, and Carter used the dust it kicked up to escape. "Hope… the droid is broken." Hope sighed with relief, "Good, as long as it's over and your OK, I'm good with that." In the observation tower, General Lyndon turned to Arthur with an angry look. "Arthur Hart, from what I have seen of this droid in battle, which wasn't much, I am afraid to tell you that you will NOT be getting the contract any time soon. Men, escort Mr. Hart to his car." The General walked away to deal with Carter as Arthur was being escorted out of the building. Carter was gone before the General was able to catch up with him.

choice. He moaned about it being Taco day in the cafeteria and bolted from the room. The teacher chuckled saying "poor kid, I can sympathize with him".

Carter rushed outside and flew off towards the labs. When he got there and walked inside the storage facility he saw the mech digging through some crates. "Who is this guy and why does Hall Industries have a battle mech, they don't have weapons. Laura has some explaining to do." He turned and when he did he kicked a wrench and flinched at the loud noise. "Oh no." The mech turned around and walked up to him. "You shouldn't be here, boy!" Carter backed up and asked, "Where's Laura and all the other scientists?" The mech grabbed him "Don't be a hero kid, it could get you killed!" He threw Carter into a pile of empty crates. He landed on his bad shoulder that was already sore from the previous day. He hurried off and snuck into a lab where Laura was helping another scientist who appeared to have a broken arm. She looked over at Carter and ran to him and gave him a hug. "Carter.... what are you doing here, it isn't safe." Carted backed up and looked at her. "I could ask you the same thing. Why haven't you left yet? Better yet, why does that battle mech have the Hall Industry logo on it?" Laura looked away as the other scientists quietly walked out of the lab. "I have valuable research here Carter, and that mech was meant to be part of a local militia force in case of an attack and that man piloting it is Arthur Hart. He came into work today, put it on and started tearing through everything before I had a chance to fire him." Laura noticed Carter had a bruise on his left shoulder. She grabbed a device and when she pointed it at his shoulder a blue light came on and his shoulder instantly felt better. "What is that thing?" Laura explained it is a new laser designed to accelerate tissue and muscle repair and that she was looking to mass produce it once it was approved by the FDA. Great, but first things first, how do I stop that mech." Carter asked. "I am not sure, I never thought to design a failsafe for it and I can't think of any structural weakness. Here, let's try this." She handed him an ear com and he put it in his ear and walked out with a disapproving look. Carters idea was to just hit the mech until it broke. He ran up behind it and jumped on its back. He tried to punch through the metal but when his hand hit it his arm shot back, and he groaned from the pain in his hand. "You dolt, this armor is made from a titanium alloy, you're not getting through it no matter what you do." Arthur than activated the defense system which threw Carter to the floor. Arthur picked him up and looked into his eyes, "It was you wasn't it….at the test site?" Carter tried to wriggle himself free from his grasp. "What are you talking about?" Arthur chuckled evilly and said, "I am going to enjoy experimenting on you kid." Just than a voice rang out from across the room "Hart! Leave him alone!" Arthur turned and saw Laura, he is not a part of this, I am! Arthur walked up to Laura and as she was turning to run he grabbed her. Don't you hurt her! The harder Carter struggled to get free the tighter Arthur squeezed. Laura looked at Arthur with a sorrowful look. "Why Arthur? Why are you doing this? You were one of my best workers, my friend." Arthur squeezed a little harder and asked "was I Laura?! Was I?! You gave that snot nosed kid more privileges around the lab than you gave me. I worked all day and all night to get to where I was, and you let her waltz around everywhere, touching everything, messing with all the other scientists!" Laura snapped back "she is my daughter and she is brilliant, that is why I gave her those privileges!" Arthur squeezed harder and she cried out in pain. "Stop it" Carter yelled. Carter started to strain and fight until finally the mechs fingers started to open. Carter forced the hand open that was holding him and yanked the mech down towards him damaging the spinal path way that it used to power the joints. Carter then swung the mech around and tossed it into some shelves of heavy equipment. He covered Laura as the mech

SECRETS

A few days later when Laura could go home, Maria and Hope had a welcome home cake ready for her. "Did you girls make this?" Hope and Maria just looked at each other until Carter admitted that he got the cake from the store. "They tried to make one, but they almost burnt the house down in the process." They all laughed. "It's the thought that counts" said Laura. They all hugged and ate cake.

Later that night, Carter walked up to Laura as she was putting a jacket on. "More secrets?" he asked. "W-what….no no…. I just…. I uhm-." Carter walked away upset and she went to the lab. While she was there she opened a hidden panel and entered a code. "Hope isn't allowed everywhere in the lab". She walked down a hidden passage that opened into another lab. Laura walked up to an obelisk. "Shep, have you decoded the words on this obelisk yet?" A monitor turned on with Shep's face. "Yes, I have." It says, "the Cosmic Warrior will reign and revive his race with the orb of life". I am unsure of the rest. "I will continue to decode the rest of the meaning. Laura nodded and walked away. She could not help but think this obelisk had something to do with Carters powers since she found it in a hidden room in his parent's basement after their deaths.

The next day in school, Carter and Maria were in gym class playing dodgeball. Carter was still upset about the mech and the secrets Laura has been keeping from them. He felt like they deserved to know, especially Hope who was basically her prodigal apprentice. Carter caught one of the dodgeballs and chucked it aimlessly and hit Maria in the gut and she fell over. Everyone ran to her. "Maria! I am so sorry, I…. I didn't mean to throw it that hard?" One of the girls helped her up as the gym teacher walked over. "CARTER, Locker room, now!" "You're staying there until the end of class to cool off!" Carter hung his head low as he walked off. When he approached one of the benches, his head started pounding and the room began to blur and spin. Everything started to fade in and out of black. He stumbled and fell on the bench and rolled off grabbing his head. The pain was the worst he had ever felt. White light began to emanate from his body.

Meanwhile, at the secret lab, the obelisk began to do the same thing. Alarms started blaring as the energy buildup in the obelisk began to reach critical levels. Hope, who was spending another day at the lab and Laura were in the main lab working when the alarms started going off. The obelisk exploded in a bright white light and a resulting shock wave shattered windows and monitors and knocked everyone back that was unlucky enough to be in its way with excessive force. Laura covered Hope as they were slammed back. Laura fell unconscious when her head slammed into the wall. When the dust settled, Hope got up and tried to wake Laura when she heard a movement come from the dark passage to the secret lab.

Lights were hanging from the ceiling and flashing while swinging back and forth. Hope slowly walked towards the noise when she saw 2 purple eyes staring back at her. Laura came to and opened her eyes in time to see Hope stepping back. The eyes began to pulsate, and Hope screamed and tried to run but the figure let out a purple flash and then Hope was gone. Laura stared in disbelief at what had just happened. Her own daughter seemingly executed on the spot. The figure stepped forward into the dim light. It was a man who looked to be in his early thirties. "I have what I need. Time for me to go I guess." Laura got up, tears in her eyes and outrage in her heart. "THAT WAS MY DAUGHTER! She didn't do anything to you!" Laura charged towards him, and he grabbed her by the throat and lifted her up. "What was that? I couldn't quite understand your choked words." His eyes were purple and full of pure malice. He tossed her aside. "I have no time for this or for you." "I have more important business to attend to...correction.... WE have more important business to attend to." He flew away, leaving Laura to curl into a ball and cry. "My baby .... why?"

Aftermath

Meanwhile, at the school Carter awoke in a destroyed locker room. The same thing that happened with the obelisk happened to him. He stood up in a daze and tried to regain his composure. He looked around and knew he had to leave quickly. He knew he needed to get to the lab, but he was not sure why. It was almost like he was being summoned there. He snuck out of the gym doors and flew to the lab. He was greeted by a grim scene. Firefighters, Police and Ambulances were flocking the lab. Carter landed discretely and ran up to the police tape. He saw paramedics and firefighters helping people out of the lab. One of those people was Laura. He ran over to her frantically. When she saw him, she hugged him tightly. When Carter did not see Hope, he knew something bad happened and they fell to their knees. His complexion went pale and tears filled his widely opened eyes.

A Game of Chess

Two nights went by and it was all he could do not to cry. Carter was always listening to the police scanner his father used to own. It was pretty banged up, but it was all he had, and he needed to find the guy who did this. It could have been argued that Maria took it the worst. She practically stopped functioning. All she did was lay in bed all day, every day. Every time Carter checked on her she had fresh tear stains on her pillow. Laura had been a wreck as well. Loud music blared from her room and a bitter smell of alcohol came from under the doorway. Carter could often hear wailing over the loud music. Muffled or not, they were gut wrenching cries. Suddenly Carter's attention was turned to the police scanner. "Krrrrrt! We have a report of a hostile superhuman attacking Fort Enderbite. Be advised, SWAT teams are in-route to provide reinforcements. Any units in the area, please respond for perimeter control. Krrrrrt" Carter grabbed his suit and flew out to the fort. When he arrived, he saw the man attacking a pinned down group of soldiers. Carter ran up behind him, grabbed his head and violently picked him up and slammed him onto the ground. He then proceeded to beat him relentlessly and quickly. The man grabbed his wrists and stopped the beating short. "Foolish boy, you shouldn't have come.... wait, those eyes...fascinating." He kicked Carter in the stomach and shoved him onto the ground and placed his knee on his chest and pushed down. "Those eyes.... yes, yes, it's you, the other warrior." Carter was able to mutter a few words. "W-What are you talking about.... I am not a warrior." The man got off Carter and set him on his feet, only to backhand him and knock him down to the ground and kick him in the stomach. Carter laid there in pain. The soldiers came out of cover to open fire, but the man shot them back with a concussive blast before they could do anything. "You're fighting for the wrong team boy. You belong on my side. The side that will revive your race." He let Carter get up and Carter immediately swung at him, but he dodged it and punched Carter in the back and he fell over. ".... who are you?" Carter asked with anger in his voice. "I am Zed of the Cosmii and you are of Cosmii descent as well. It's in your genetic coding....... somewhere. Far into the past, a Cosmii left our home world, before we drove it to its demise, and came here and found herself a human spouse. Though it was foolish of her to do so. Cosmii live so much longer than humans.......a trait you most likely do not possess due to you having more human DNA than Cosmii." Carter stood up holding his back. "I don't want anything to do with your race. Especially if it means hurting innocent people.... like that girl ... The girl you murdered in cold blood!" Zed looked confused at first, but then figured out that he meant Hope and he began to laugh. "What's so funny?" Carter asked between clenched teeth. "You think I murdered her? What a laugh! Allow me to show you what I really did with her." He snapped his fingers and just then a woman vaulted off Carters shoulders and landed between him and Zed. When she turned around, she revealed an aged Hope, about 21 years old with long black hair and purple eyes. She wore the same black armor as Zed. Carter stepped back in disbelief. "You..... what did you do to her?" Zed chuckled. "I made her my pawn. All it took was a little power from an ancient relic of our race." He pulled out a white shining crystal. "Behold, the Cosmic Crystal. It contains unbelievable power. Unfortunately, I cannot access all of it. Only the chosen Cosmic Warrior can utilize all the power. But he, or she, isn't around it seems." The crystal turned black. "But with enough focus, willpower and desire to do what I wish, I can use a small portion of its power..... not that any of this information will help you in any way. You won't live long enough to utilize it. Pawn destroy him." Hope took a battle stance and Carter backed away. "Hope, I know you don't want to do this. Come on Hope, you remember me, right? Right?!" Hope darted at him and began to ruthlessly attack him. All Carter could do is dodge and block when he could. Zed watched in amusement. "Come on Hope, the power is corrupting you, fight it. I know you are smart enough. I know you are strong enough. Please fight—AH!" Hope had punched Carter in the stomach, causing him to keel over. She went to deliver the final blow, but Zed stopped her. "Now, pawn, no need to sully your hands with his blood. He is entirely to weak. To kill him like this would be...dishonorable. Besides, we may be able to use him later, if he ever comes to his senses. Let's leave him to writhe in his own failure." Hope backed away and they flew off. General Lyndon walked up to Carter who laid on the ground. "... Come on soldier, lets patch you up." Some soldiers walked up and carried Carter to the infirmary to administer first aid.

Later that night, Carter awoke in the base infirmary. "Well, well, well. Good morning sleepy head. Carter sat up and looked to see General Lyndon sitting in the corner. He then grabbed his

ZEDS HOME BASE

Zed and Hope were up in space approaching a new space station the U.S Government set up for research purposes. "With the right modifications, this station will suit our cause just fine…. how are you doing pawn? Are you able to breathe up here?" He turned to check on Hope and she was fine. I was concerned that the crystal wouldn't give you the ability I have. I get very lonely, especially after being trapped in that obelisk for a few millennia. My dreams were the only things that kept me sane. They continued to approach the station. "Now, pawn, would you care to take the lead?" A helmet covered Hopes face. She ripped off an opening hatch. They entered the airlock and opened the next hatch and walked in. A seal went down behind them and an alarm blared loudly. Zed glared at her. "I am happy you found a quick way in, but I wanted something more subtle." People started running towards them. "Pawn take care of them, I am going for a walk." Hope started towards them while Zed went to the control room. "Let's see now.... ah, zero gravity." He turned off the gravity, he would mess with the power core later. Just then, Hope floated in. "Oh, you're done already". It didn't take as long as I expected. Good work Pawn." He heard groaning coming from down the hall. "Alive? Well, I guess I did say to be more subtle. Oh well, shove them all in the escape pods and then we may leave." Hope did as she was told, and they left to go steal some supplies they would need for their big plan.

Hope is Alive

Later that night, Carter finally returned home to see Maria making Laura some coffee. Laura was looking a little green. She looked at Carter as he walked up to the table. "Hey…" Carter dropped the photos Lyndon gave him on the table in front of her. "That's the man Mom described, but who's the girl?" asked Maria. "Check out the close up." He pulled the picture out from the bottom of the pile and handed it to them. They were still confused. "That is the squirt." Maria looked at him with an angry expression. "That is not funny carter." Laura's eyes started to water. "Good, its no supposed to be, I'm serious. That's her, he corrupted her by dark power and somehow aged her but it's her. That guy, Zed, admitted it was her. He needed a pawn and she was the first person he saw." Laura got up. "We…we need to go find her." Carter took her arm and Maria took the other. "You aren't going anywhere." Carter replied. "You need sleep, you need a bath and you need to eat something. I will go and look for Hope and Zed." Maria ran after him before he flew off. "Wait, you can't go alone......I know you lost that fight from the pictures. You need help Carter." Carter turned to her and with a sarcastic tone said "Sure....I'll just call up the Avengers or the X-men. Oh wait, I can't.... they're not real. I am the only one who can do this Maria." Maria grabbed his hand. "There has got to be someone who can help you. You don't even know where to start looking for them. Please, just come back in and rest, your still injured." As Carter's adrenaline wore down he fainted into Maria's arms. She took him inside and laid him in his bed then sat in the chair beside him and they both slept. When she awoke an hour later to check on him, he was still fast asleep. She went downstairs to make some tea and turned on the news and she saw Hope and Zed robbing another tech company. She was full of disbelief when she saw them hurting innocent people including police and the authorities. Zed had turned her baby sister into a monster. Hope's eyes were so cold and unfeeling. It broke Maria's heart to see her this way. Carter walked downstairs and turned the TV off and Maria flew into his arms, crying uncontrollably. "How could he do that to her? How could he do that!? She is just a little girl." Carter comforted her the best he could, but he was hurting also. "I promise, I will get her back and bring her home where she belongs." They sat down, and Carter let Maria cling to him and cry it out the rest of the night. She finally cried herself to sleep in his arms. He felt her sorrow and it pained him. It made him angry that Zed could inflict so much pain on the people he loved without even touching them. There didn't even seem to be a reason for him to do this other than he just wanted to. Carter laid on the couch all night with Maria clinging to him. Every now and then he would awake to her whimpering in her sleep. He felt conflicted about what he should do. Part of him wanted to stay and comfort Maria and Laura and another part wanted to go find Zed and Hope. He was at an impasse.

BREAKING FREE

Meanwhile, Zed and Hope were working up at the space station. Hope was messing around with the power core as Zed looked for food. He started in the pantry and was throwing packets of astronaut food behind him. "Food.... food.... FOOD! Where is the food!? Surely these humans need sustenance, but all that's here are these packets of.... of...garbage!" He squeezed a packet of applesauce so hard it popped and went all over his face. "GAH! Elders help me with my patience for I am losing EVERY LAST OUNCE OF IT!" Zed turned around to see Hope floating around with a wrench in her hand. "Pawn! Don't just sit there, fetch me a rag!" Hope did as she was told. He wiped his face and cursed under his breath. "If you reached a stopping point in your work join me on the surface below. We are going out for food." He flew down and Hope followed. When they arrived, they were in New York City and they blasted their way into a bakery. "Dine while you can Pawn, we are not staying long." He ate fiercely, digging into donuts, cakes and entire loaves of bread while Hope ate at a more mannerly pace. When Zed was done eating he looked around for Hope, but she was gone. "Pawn, Pawn, where did you go? He heard a door open as she walked out of a rest room. "Notify me when you wander off like that...wait...you wandered off? How did you do that? Perhaps your body's needs trigger a part of your mind that guides you to fulfilling that need.... fascinating." Hope walked over to a cooler of soda and water and hesitated on which to grab. "My pawn is thinking on her own.... this worries me. Pawn grab your drink, we are going back to the station." Hope grabbed a water and flew off with him.

The next day Carter woke up and went to the kitchen to see Maria and Laura sitting at the table drinking some tea. Carter sat with them in silence for a few minutes. Maria was first to speak. "Carter, can you glow?" Carter looked at her with a confused expression on his face. I woke up this morning and my hand was glowing, and I felt at peace, oddly at peace...with everything that's going on. Then you started having a bad dream and I felt fear, lots of fear." Carter looked up at Laura and they both shrugged. "Well, um, maybe we are so close that we are bonded together.... maybe when one of us sees the other in pain or discomfort we feel the others pain." As for the glowing, maybe it was just blurry morning vision." Maria shook her head. "No...that is not it.... watch." She put her hand on Laura's shoulder and it started glowing. She thought of the fun times she had playing with Hope and they both smiled and giggled, but then they turned to frowns and tears. Carter wasn't sure what to make of it. It's like it happens when you both have intense feelings. "Maybe, maybe we need to get to the lab and run some tests." Laura stood up and took them out to the shed behind the house. She opened a security panel and typed in a code and another panel opened. It was a bio scanner. She placed her hand on it and the door opened and there was a staircase going to an underground lab. "When were you going to tell us about this?" Carter asked. Laura just looked at him and with a somber tone said, "When it was done." Carter felt like a jerk and they walked down into the lab together. "Maria, go place your hand on that blue panel over there...Carter, you do the same." Maria and Carter did as they were told. Laura scanned both of their hands into the system. After some time, the computer came back with results. Maria's body was generating energy that was like Carter's just not as strong. "This is strange, Maria has a very similar energy signature as Carter... but how? "Laura sat down to think, and Maria and Carter walked over to her. Carter was the first to speak. "Are my powers, I don't know, radioactive?" Laura looked at him and shrugged. "I guess, that's all I can label them as..... are you suggesting that all the time you spend with Maria gave her some of your energy or powers?" Carter shrugged...maybe. Laura slumped back in her chair and thought about it.

FORCED HANDS

Later that night, Carter ran out to go confront Zed and Hope again. According to the scanner, they were breaking into a steel mill a few towns over. While Hope was dealing with the workers and the authorities, Zed was busy with one of his schemes. He was trying to make something from the molten metal at the mill. He carved a mold of a sword into a steel slab and poured molten steel into the mold and waited for it to harden before he could get to work. Meanwhile, Carter landed outside to see Hope taking care of some police officers. "Hope...stop this, right now." Hope dropped the officer and walked up to Carter. "Please Hope, come home to your family...you don't have to be his puppet. You must fight his control. You can do it, I know you can." Hope started to charge towards him and he charged towards her and they clashed.

In the mill, Zed's sword molding had cooled enough for him to work with it. He removed the sword while the fighting went on outside. "Blast it, that noise out there is distracting me. My pawn shouldn't be having any trouble with those weak humans..... what is going on." He continued working trusting hope could handle the situation.

Outside, Hope and Carters battle was heating up. She was lightning fast and hit like a freight train. Carter was out of options, he did not want to fight her with all his strength, but it was getting hard to avoid it. Hitting a girl just didn't feel right. "Sorry Hope." He countered one of her strikes with a punch to her face. She stumbled back and continued fighting. After several minutes of fighting Carter tackled her through several walls and they stopped in the same room as Zed. Carter looked up at him and he was kicked in the face and knocked out.

When he came to, he was in a dark room with two people standing over him and a bright light shining in his eyes. When his vision cleared, he realized they were a detective and an officer. "What's going on?" he asked nervously as he tried to move his hands, but they were cuffed. He decided to keep them on for now. The detective answered him "We would like to ask you the same thing. Who are you and who are the other two that helped you into the mill?" Carters eyes widened. "Helped? I was trying to stop them!" The detective stepped back. "A likely story. It was probably a diversion, so the other guy could do this." He slapped a picture of the steel block Zed used for his sword down in front of Carter. Carter was starting to think there was no way of getting out of this but then General Lyndon opened the door. "That will be enough detective. I have my own questions for this boy. After all, he was on my military base yesterday when these two struck there and I would like to ask him a few more questions. The answers may be classified so I will have to ask you to clear the room." The detective shook his head and stormed out in a huff. The officer followed. General Lyndon gave Carter his mask and they left and climbed into a Humvee waiting outside. On their way back, Lyndon spoke. "I think this makes us pretty much even for you saving my men.... but now I have a favor to ask you." Carter looked over at him, "What is it?" he asked. Lyndon pulled out a water bottle and took a drink. "I need your help in finding out what those two freaks want with the U.S. Government research station and a couple million dollars' worth of highly classified technology." Carter thought for a moment and answered, "Your guess is as good as mine sir, but maybe there is someone who might know something." Carter pulled out his cellphone and placed a call.

REALIZATIONS

Back at the manor, Laura was sitting in her lab with an ice pack on her head. "I hate myself for doing this." Maria came by with a glass of ice water and set it by her, only for Laura to pick it up and press it against her forehead instead of drinking it. She still looked sick as a dog. Just then, Maria's phone rang. It was Carter. Carter's voice sounded urgent "Maria, quick put your mother on." Maria gave the phone to Laura. "What now?" She sounded even worse than she did a few seconds ago. "Laura did Zed say anything when he took Hope from the lab, or is there any information you have that could explain his motives?" Laura put the phone down and thought for a moment and then picked it back up. "He was stuck in some sort of obelisk. It exploded but I remember what it said. It said.... uh.... The Cosmic, something will rise and.... something about the orb of life. "Everything is so foggy right now." She rubbed her temples. "OK...General Lyndon will be sending you a list of what Zed has stolen so far. Try to piece together what he is making. I have to go now, I'll talk to you in a bit." He hung up and Laura's head fell on the desk...." joy!"

Confrontation

Meanwhile, Carter and General Lyndon drove into the military base and they walked up to a ship. It was somewhat like VTOL, but built for transport, not combat. "What are we doing here?" Carter asked, scratching his head. "We are heading to a top secret base a couple hundred miles out of the county in what we call "no man's land." They boarded the ship and strapped in. "Just so you know, I am not good with planes?" Carter gripped his straps nervously. "You can fly, how is a plane any different?" Carter glared at him. "It just is!" he spoke in a defensive tone. The pilot shot back at them saying "You know you're more likely to get struck by lightning than to die in one of these things, right?" Carter felt sick to his stomach and said, "that doesn't help". They took off and about 10 minutes later, Carters phone rang. "Those aren't very secure you know." Lyndon warned him. Carter shrugged it off saying that no one knew he was there or even what he was for that matter, and he answered the phone. Before he could say anything Laura immediately started going off. He had to pull the phone away from his ear she was yelling so loud. "Laura, hold on…h-hold on. Laura! I can barely understand you, talk slower…. and quieter." Laura took deep breaths and calmed down. "Carter, those parts that Zed stole, they are equipment that can make a few things, but the one is completely terrifying. He is building a laser. If he can mount it to a satellite or the research station up in space, it could do major damage. He could strike anywhere he wanted with enough power to man a giant reactor" Carter cut her off. "or with that crystal of his…he could destroy a lot more than a few buildings." Cater went pale. Lyndon could only imagine what they were talking about to scare Carter like this. "Carter, you have to stop him….and you have to bring my baby home and the "whole orb of life" that was mentioned on the obelisk…. I think it means Earth." Carter nodded and hung up. "We need to get to Zed…fast." Lyndon nodded. "Good thing we have a way to get you to him. He is up in space right now, the eggheads tracked him down." The pilot yelled back at them. "Sir! We are approaching the facility." Carter just looked at Lyndon who had a big smirk. "Hope you get your space legs quick." He chuckled. They went inside to set Carter up for space travel. A three-seater shuttle awaited him. "is that a…a…uh…what is that exactly?" Lyndon scratched his head. "It's sort of like a ship you see in something like Star Wars or Star Trek…. minus the guns." Carter nodded and stared up in amazement. Two people in militarized astronaut suits passed him. A woman and a man. "Are you ready small fry?" the man teased. The woman elbowed him. "Be nice, he is risking his life for the whole world." She put a hand on Carters shoulder. "Ignore Doof, he is a…. well…. a doofus." Carter snickered at his name. His name tag literally said "Doof." Doof went up to the shuttle obviously annoyed and hopped in. "My name is Carol. What's your name?" Carter shook her hand. "Carter" Carol walked ahead and motioned him to follow. "Well, Carter, let's get going." She hopped into her seat leaving the middle open for Carter. Carter hopped in the middle and the hatch went over them. Doof was shocked Carter didn't get a space suit. "What about his space suit?" he asked. "I have been up where planes fly, and breathing has never been an issue for me. I will be fine." Doof shrugged and initiated the launch sequence. "Lyndon warned us you were different". They all strapped in and prepared for the launch. After a brief time, the roar of the engines blocked out the other sounds. They even blocked out any thought that might have run through their heads. Within seconds, they were flying through the sky and a little more than a minute later, they were in space. The booster rockets detached, and the shuttles main thrusters engaged, and they flew to the research station.

Up at the space station, Zed and Hope were working on the laser, but they were having trouble. "Why isn't this working?" Everything is set up correctly, but the laser isn't receiving any of the crystals power." He removed the crystal from the device. "Don't tell me I have to do it manually." Hope tapped his shoulder and pointed towards the door. "What is it pawn? Are you telling me to leave? "Wait, what is out there"? He ran out to the window and saw Carter, Doof and Carol exiting their shuttle down by the destroyed air lock. Carter pried the seal open and Carol and Doof flew through and he jumped in as well, barely avoiding the seal. "Good job kid" Doof slapped his back. "Let's get going." Carol readied a rifle and walked on ahead of them. Zed growled at this and barked at Hope. "DESTROY THEM AT ONCE!" Hope flew down quickly and flew straight for Carter. He ducked, and she slammed right into a wall. While she was getting up Carol ran up to her and hit her hard with the butt of her rifle. Carter pulled her away. "Stop, don't hurt her!" He rolled her over on her back.

"She doesn't know what she is doing. She is his puppet." Carol stepped towards him. "I know you are trying to be a hero Carter, but we have to do what we have to do to survive this." Carter stood up and blocked Hope with his body. "No. You're not touching her." Carol went to bark at him but Doof grabbed her shoulder and held her back. "Just drop it Carol......maybe there is a way to fix her. Nobody has to die today." Carol shrugged him off and stormed away. As she stomped away Hope's eyes shot open and she grabbed Carters leg and swung him right into Doof. Carol turned to shoot but Hope was too fast, she slapped the rifle out of her hands and grabbed her throat. Carter got up and ran towards her. "Hope! Stop!" Hope threw Carol at him. He ducked, and she hit Doof just as he got to his feet, knocking him down again. "Hope, please stop! This isn't you. You must remember. If you just try, I know you will remember me. He took off his mask as Hope approached him. "Remember Maria, remember your Mom, Laura. Remember your love for Hall Industries and the lab. Come on Squirt don't do this" She stopped walking and her glare turned to an innocent look. "I know you are not much of Squirt now, but...you will always be Hope Hall. That little munchkin who somehow always managed to get me to share half a candy bar with her." He slowly approached her. "Do you....do you remember yet?" He held out his hand to her. Carol and Doof watched intently. Hope slowly moved her arm and placed her hand over his. Her metal gauntlet creaked as she slowly wrapped her hand around his. "You do remember, don't you?" Carter smiled brightly. Just then Zed yelled from across the room. "So, you managed to break my control. You will pay for that insufferable vermin." Hope charged at Zed only to get blasted into the wall. "I will kill you for betraying me." Carter charged at him. "LEAVE HER ALONE!" He went to punch Zed, but Zed quickly grabbed Carters wrist and squeezed it. Doof ran at him. Zed swung Carter around and threw him into

Doof and they both crashed into Carol. Doof was getting a little tired of this scenario. Carter groaned in pain as he heard slight cracks in his wrist. "Does that hurt boy? Don't worry, it won't for long…because you will be distracted by all the other pain I will inflict upon you!" He punched Carter with his other hand. "You will suffer by my hand, I will never let you die. You will suffer in every way imaginable. I will beat you and then destroy your friends and family in front of you starting with my pawn." Carter looked at him with rage in his eyes and he got to his feet, clenching the fist that was held by Zed. "Quit calling her that"! He pushed his hand back and delivered a swift left hook, sending Zed flying into a window which cracked. "Don't you EVER threaten the people I care for again!" He uppercut Zed, sending him flying back and the Cosmii Crystal flew off him. Carter grabbed it and tossed it to Doof who fumbled with it but caught it. Carter approached Zed who shot him back with a powerful energy blast. "FIRE IN THE HOLE!" Doof threw a grenade and Carol threw a flashbang, first Zed was stunned, then the grenade went off and it sent him flying back. The window Zeds head hit broke and started sucking air out. Carol and Doof grabbed Hope and Carter and ran to the air lock but it was still sealed. "Stand back." Carol threw a remote bomb on the seal and then hid behind a wall. She detonated it and the seal was opened and they were all sucked out into space near the shuttle. Doof opened the hatch and they all piled in for the return trip to Earth.

was with Carter. She was different, but she was still her daughter. Alive and unharmed, at least on the outside. Laura walked up to her. "H-Hope...do you....do you remember me?" Hope nodded. "Mom" Carter stepped back as Laura hugged her as tight as she could, crying the whole time. Maria joined in and she pulled Carter into their group hug. Hope was confused and a little distraught, but she hugged back, tearing up herself but remaining quiet. She couldn't believe they were willing to forgive who she had become and what she had done. She just hoped that someday she could learn to forgive herself.

Later that night, bits and pieces of Hopes armor laid on the floor and she slept on the couch. It was the first time she was able to really rest since Zed corrupted her. "What is that suit she was wearing? Is it like chainmail?" Carter scratched his head as he examined the fabric. "Well, her armor IS metal. If she gets caught in a fire trap or if it breaks, it will hurt her." Carter nodded as Laura was coming in. She sat by Hope and examined her jet-black shoulder length hair. Her hair was originally blonde and short. She noticed Carter had the Cosmic Crystal in his hand. It pulsated yellow. "Carter...can you fix her with that?" "I don't really know anything about this thing, but I feel like I should." He looked at it and held it up and concentrated hard. Hope glowed and the shard did as well. Slowly, she reverted to her normal self. Her hair was short again and returned to its original blonde color, and her size shrunk as well. She was now the child she was before Zed corrupted her, at least on the outside. Carter's energy was drained, he was sweating and shaking. Carter tried to leave to give them all some peace and quiet and some alone time, but they insisted he stay, so he did. Later that night while everyone slept, Carter heard a high-pitched squeak and then a thud. He shot up to see Hope trying to get used to her body again. She was standing up on shaky legs. They were much shorter and weaker than they were after Zed changed her. Carter got up and helped support her. "Carter, I am so sorry, I didn't mean to wake you." Carter shook his head. "Its fine, I wasn't really asleep anyway...how do you feel?" Hope struggled to take a few steps. "Not as strong as I was before.... but I will be OK." "Thank you, Carter." He patted her head and helped her take a few steps before she passed out in his arms, sound asleep. He laid her beside Laura as he took his place on the other side of the couch.

Vengeance

Meanwhile, up in the research station, all gravity was off due to the window being broken from the fight that transpired. His vision was blurry, and the left side of his head was covered in blood. His vision eventually cleared, and he rushed to a bathroom to look in a mirror and he saw the whole left side of his face was scratched from grenade shrapnel, and his eye was too damaged to ever be used again. He let out a roar of pain, rage and sorrow. "GYYAAAAHHHHH! YOU SWIIINNEE! I WILL GET EVEN WITH EVERY LAST ONE OF YOU!" Black fire emanated from Zeds body. He was full of pure, unbridled rage. This fire expanded and in an instant, consumed the station and tore it to pieces. He shouted out to Earth still screaming. "ALL WILL BURN BEFORE ME."

Meanwhile, back at the manor, Carter shot up after just falling asleep, he was not sure what woke him, but somehow, he knew what he sensed was Zeds pain and rage…. he was just not sure how. He could feel the hate and the bloodlust and the need for revenge. Carter was terrified, he immediately woke everyone up and locked them in the underground lab outback. Maria pounded on the locked door. "CARTER, you let me out of here. CARTER…. let me out." Carter walked away to confront Zed. When they came face to face, Carter was horrified at Zeds disfigured face. He recognized that sense of anger and rage that woke him. "Zed…. what happened to you? It looks like you lost a fight". In a split second, Carter was being held up by his shirt and found himself at Zeds mercy. "You did this…YOU DID THIS TO ME. You and those insufferable humans. Carter kicked him away. "You did that to yourself. You were trying to blow up the planet." Zed backhanded Carter and knocked him into the dirt and he dropped straight down on him. "I was trying to save my race…OUR race, but now all I want is to get my revenge on you. You ruined my face and after I get my revenge on you I will destroy this planet by eviscerating its core!"

Back at the lab, Laura was desperately trying to get something done on the lower level while Hope moped around, and Maria tried to get the door open. "Will you stop…its not opening, he busted the lock, so we couldn't get out." Hopes voice was dull and tired. This is all my fault. Maria didn't listen and continued to try and pry it open. Her powers were flaring up again. The door creaked and drew Hopes attention before it was ripped right off its hinges and almost flattened her. Luckily, she jumped out of the way in time. "MARIA, how in the world did you do that? Look at you, you are glowing!" Maria was gone. She ran out to go find and help Carter. Hope just stared at the doorway in awe as Laura walked up to her. She had a large device in her hand. "Whoa, Mom. What is this thing? Is that a gun?" Laura nodded…." of sorts…it's supposed to drain power from anything electronic, like if something malfunctions and you cannot shut it down. I have modified it to drain powers like Carter's though. It should work on Zed. Those two are somehow connected." Just then there was a loud boom outside. When they ran out they saw Zed pinning Carter down and ruthlessly beating him. Carter blocked as many blows as he could, but it felt like his arms were about to break. "I WILL TRIUMPH!" Maria grabbed the device from Laura and jumped on Zeds back and grabbed his face. Gray veins appeared on him and he grew weak. Maria was draining his energy. "S-stop.... please, have mercy." Maria had fire in her eyes, she felt his rage. "NEVER!" Zed struggled to remove her before he fell over and passed out. Black fire appeared on her skin and her eyes turned black as she leveled an energy blast at him. She somehow seemed to absorb his dark energy the same way she absorbed Carters clean energy. Carter grabbed her hand. "Maria don't do this, please." Maria glared at him, but he was not scared. He gently pushed her arm down and took her hand and with his other, pulled her into a hug. Her black fire faded, her eyes went back to normal and all the energy she stole from Zed went right back into him. He jumped up and shot Carter in the back with an energy blast and he flew forward, taking Maria with him. Laura ran up and Zed shot her in the leg and she dropped to the ground and so did the gun. Zed proceeded to crush it with his foot and then he rested his other foot on her head. "Did you see what I did to your gun, human? I can do the same thing to you." Hope ran up behind him. "Leave my Mama alone!" Zed swiped his arm through the air and a shockwave sent her back. Carter laid in the dirt and he heard and felt all this happening. "Why...why can't I beat you.... why can't I get stronger?" He punched the dirt. "I cannot let this happen." He stood up and the crystal, which was in his pocket, began to glow bright blue. "I—I won't let this happen? I won't let you hurt innocent people anymore. Especially not the ones I

About the Author

Raymond Henry, author of "Cosmic Warrior" grew up in a small town in Pennsylvania. He was interested in writing and super heroes at a young age, so it was no surprise when he combined the two and created Carter, the Cosmic Warrior in the 10th grade. He wants to share Carter's exploits with everyone so grab a chair and enjoy.

Printed in the United States
By Bookmasters